S0-BFD-431

Date D

FE

THE EVIL PEN PAL

titles in Large-Print Editions:

CHOOSE YOUR OWN NIGHTMARE #14

THE EVIL PEN PAL

by Laban Carrick Hill

Illustrated by Bill Schmidt

An R. A. Montgomery Book

Gareth Stevens Publishing
MILWAUKEE

For a free color catalog describing Gareth Stevens' list of high-quality books and multimedia programs, call 1-800-542-2595 (USA) or 1-800-461-9120 (Canada). Gareth Stevens Publishing's Fax: (414) 225-0377. See our catalog, too, on the World Wide Web: http://gsinc.com

Library of Congress Cataloging-in-Publication Data

Hill, Laban Carrick.
    The evil pen pal / by Laban Carrick Hill ; illustrated by Bill Schmidt.
      p. cm. — (Choose your own nightmare; #14)
    Summary: The reader makes choices that control the outcome of a visit from pen pal Billy, who is not the way he seemed in his letters.
    ISBN 0-8368-2071-1 (lib. bdg.)
    1. Plot-your-own stories. [1. Horror stories. 2. Pen pals—Fiction. 3. Plot-your-own stories.] I. Schmidt, Bill, ill. II. Title. III. Series.
PZ7.H55286Ev   1998
[Fic]—dc21   97-39603

This edition first published in 1998 by
Gareth Stevens Publishing
1555 North RiverCenter Drive, Suite 201
Milwaukee, Wisconsin 53212 USA

Printed in the United States of America

1 2 3 4 5 6 7 8 9 02 01 00 99 98

The evil pen pal

54334

THE EVIL PEN PAL

WARNING!

You have probably read books where scary things happen to people. Well, in *Choose Your Own Nightmare,* you're right in the middle of the action. The scary things are happening to you!

Having a pen pal is really cool. You love getting mail with your name on it. But is meeting your pen pal in person a good idea? You'll find out in this scary story.

Don't forget—YOU control your fate. Only you can decide what happens. Follow the instructions at the bottom of each page. The thrills and chills that happen to you will depend on your choices!

So what are you waiting for? It's time to meet your pen pal. Cross your fingers, turn to page 1, and get ready to . . . *CHOOSE YOUR OWN NIGHTMARE*!

"Hey Mom! Guess what?"

"If you want to speak to me, you'll have to come downstairs!" your mom calls.

Thump! Thump! Thump! You bound down the stairs, ready to burst with excitement.

"And how often do I have to tell you not to run around the house like a herd of elephants?"

You ignore her. "Here. Read." You hand her a piece of paper. She's not wearing her reading glasses, so she has to hold it at arm's length. "Hmmm," she answers.

"So what do you think?"

"Um," your mom says thoughtfully. "I don't know. I can't read the handwriting."

You snatch the letter from her. "I'll read it to you. It's from Billy, in Florida. You know, my pen pal," you remind her.

"Read it," your mom says.

" 'My mom and dad say I can come up and visit for a week. What do you think? Let me know when school break is, okay?' "

You look up from the letter expectantly. "Can he come, Mom? Please, please, pleeeeeeeezzz!"

Find out if Billy can come on page 2.

2

"Well, I suppose it would be okay," your mom says slowly. "You *are* going to be off from school."

"All right!" you yell, dashing upstairs to your room. You want to get your answer in the mail right away. But you run into your older brother, Mike, first.

"I know something you don't," Mike brags.

"Leave me alone," you say, trying to slide by.

"But this is important," he says, pushing you against the hall wall. "It's about your pen pal Billy."

"You don't have anything to tell me about Billy," you say.

"Yeah, I do," he says.

"Leave me alone," you say, pushing past him into your room. You slam the door in his face.

You can hear Mike breathing heavily on the other side of the door. "One more chance," Mike whispers. "Then it's going down the toilet."

You can't stand it when Mike taunts you. He always knows how to get under your skin.

Hurry to page 3 if you've got to know what he has to say.

Flip to page 68 if you plan to ignore Mike as usual.

You know you can't ignore Mike no matter how much you want to. He always wins. "Someday . . . ," you mutter under your breath, "you're going to get what's coming to you."

You jerk the door open.

Mike is standing there holding a smudged envelope between his thumb and forefinger. You grab it and slam the door in his face with a sense of satisfaction. "Go away!" you shout.

The envelope is folded in half. It looks as if it's been in someone's pocket for weeks. Knowing Mike, it could have been. Especially since it's already been opened.

You slip the letter out. The ink is smudged, and the paper is wrinkled, as though someone had dropped it in water.

I hate to write this letter.

You can't make out the next few words. Then it continues:

I have to warn you. Do not let Billy come to your house. Ever! He's a mons . . .

The rest is a blur. You can't even tell who it's from. The ink bleeds all the way to the bottom of the page. You scan the letter to see when it was written, but there's no date.

Turn to page 26.

4

Sometimes it's a real drag being a kid, especially when you have to get your parents' approval to do something.

In order to convince your mom to let you call, you behave perfectly. You set the table. You pick up your room. You take out the garbage.

At supper Mike teases you about being so helpful. "You're such a weasel, always trying to look good in front of the 'rents." Mike always calls your parents the 'rents.

You slouch in your chair and play with the edge of your napkin. You don't want to pick up the bait. The last thing that will help your case is getting into a fight with Mike.

Fortunately, your dad comes to your defense. It's the first thing he's said all night. "Cut it out, Mike. You should be as helpful."

You look up and smile as nicely as you can. Your dad taking your side is a good sign.

After a few more minutes, your mom puts her fork down and looks you in the eye. "Okay," she says. "You can call Kevin."

"Yes!" You leap out of your chair.

"But . . ."

Always a "but"! Go to page 14.

Two days later, you and your parents are riding in an elevator to the seventh floor of St. William's Hospital. You're going to the psychiatric ward. You and your friends call it the "flight deck," because it's where all the crazies are located.

You're making your first visit to Billy. According to the police, when Billy ran away from your house, he stopped a car and pushed the driver out. They caught up with him a block away and brought him to the hospital. Apparently he was acting really strange.

You walk down the long, empty hallway with your parents and sign in at a desk. An orderly leads you to a visiting room, where a small boy dressed in pajamas is sitting at a table.

Hesitantly, you say, "Hi, Billy. How're you feeling?"

Billy stares ahead. He acts like he doesn't see you.

"Ahem," someone says from behind you.

Find out who on page 12.

6

"Let's go get help!" you scream, pushing Billy out the door ahead of you. He seems reluctant to leave. You can tell he wants to help your dad.

Unexpectedly, your dad grabs the guy, pulls him toward the window, then throws him on the ground.

You nudge Billy. "Guess that guy didn't know my dad has a black belt in judo."

"Really?" Billy asks excitedly.

You nod.

"Cool!" he says. "Could he show me some moves?"

"Well, maybe some basic stuff."

A chorus of horns blares. "Hey!" your dad shouts to you. "Get in the car!"

As you open the back door, the van driver hops up and gives you a shove.

Without hesitation, Billy goes for him.

Flip to page 33.

Dear Pen Pal,

What's up? Have you heard from Kevin? Not a word on this end since July. Wrote him five times since, but no answer. He's such a weird dude. First he sends us an avalanche of letters, now not a trickle. It's like the Mohave Desert. Dry as a bone.

Anyway, my hand was getting tired trying to keep up. I had a big blister on the end of my finger from holding a pencil so much . . .

If you hear from Kevin, let me know.

Your pen pal,

Sue

You try to remember what you wrote back. But you can't. And, of course, you don't keep copies of your letters. Why didn't Kevin's disappearance strike you as odd back then? You remember that you were certain a new onslaught of letters would eventually show up.

Turn to page 66.

8

You hop out of the car before your dad can say anything.

"Billy?" you call to the boy. You yell out who you are.

He turns. There's a strange, detached look in his eyes. Then a wide smile of recognition spreads across his face. "Hey, great to see you!" He runs over to you.

As he climbs into the backseat, Billy gives you a friendly slap on the shoulder. He seems really excited and happy. "Let's get out of here," he says to your dad.

"Not a chance, Billy," your dad says. "We're trapped." He points to the cars lined up behind and in front.

You hop out and get in the back with Billy. "How was the flight?"

"Yeah," your dad says. "And what's all the commotion at the terminal?"

Billy shrugs as he slides low in his seat. "Not a clue." He pauses awkwardly. "The flight was terrific. We were served peanuts, ham sandwiches, and as much soda as we wanted." He pulls a can of soda out of his pocket. "Here, I grabbed this for you."

Hurry to page 61.

"Who do you think, nimrod? I'm Billy!" the kid yells. Your eyes focus on his angry face. "You can't just blow me off. I made plans to visit you!" he continues angrily.

You hold up your hands, expecting a blow. "I'm sorry, but I didn't realize you'd be angry," you plead.

"Angry! Angry isn't the word for it!" he shouts.

Suddenly you find yourself flying through the hallway and slamming headfirst into your mother's favorite Degas reproduction. It's the one with all the ballerinas, and all you can think is how angry she's going to be. How are you going to explain *this* to her?

Then you realize something is not right. You were just tossed across the hall by a boy who is smaller than you are. And he didn't even lift a finger!

Better check out page 15.

10

It comes to you in a flash. "The library!" you shout. The library has telephone books for every part of the country.

You shove your feet into your sneakers without tying them. "Bye, Mom!" you yell. "I'm going to the library."

"It's about time," your mom answers sarcastically. "Do you know where it is?"

You ignore your mom's humor. Of course you know where the library is. You walk by it every day on your way to school. It's only two blocks away.

"That Mom," you huff. "She's a regular comic. They should put her on TV."

You hope the library is open. You remember hearing something about budget cuts. As you run up the steps, the building looks dark. But then, it always looks dark. It's an old building, and the windows are really dirty.

The lobby is a massive marble room with forty-foot ceilings. To the right is a small desk with a sign on it: INFORMATION. Behind it sits a woman in a gray suit with a pair of glasses hanging from a string around her neck. She points you in the right direction.

Head that way on page 28.

12

"He's under heavy sedation," a doctor explains as he enters the room. "The tragedy is that we can't find his parents. The address that you gave us in Florida is an empty lot. Do you know anything about him?"

"He's my pen pal. He came up for a visit," you tell him.

The doctor shakes his head and walks out of the visitors' room. "He's going to be here a long time," he says over his shoulder.

After your visit, your parents take you for a milk shake. Chocolate. You promise yourself that you will visit Billy every week, as long as he's in the hospital.

You keep your promise for a couple of months. When summer arrives, it becomes more and more difficult to tear yourself away from the games in your neighborhood. Eventually you lose track of Billy and think of him only on rare occasions.

The End

"My arm!" Mike shrieks in agony. He turns on Billy. *"How did you do that?"*

"Do what?" Billy asks innocently, the sneer vanishing from his face.

Mike drops to his knees in pain. "This!" he screams as he tries to hold up his broken arm.

Out of nowhere your dad races out and grabs Billy. Billy thrashes and spits in your dad's face like a wild animal.

"Calm down, son," your dad says soothingly. "We don't want to hurt you."

Billy squirms and throws his head back and forth. He won't give up even though he doesn't have a chance against your dad. Finally your dad picks Billy up and carries him kicking and screaming into the house.

Meanwhile, your mom has taken Mike inside. He's sitting at the kitchen table, sobbing. His arm dangles awkwardly at his side. It's a bad break. Your mom is searching frantically for the car keys to take Mike to the emergency room. The noise of the television blares over the chaotic scene.

Then suddenly everyone stops in their tracks.

Go to page 64, now!

14

"But," your mom says, "you have to clean up the supper plates first." Your parents are sneaky. They never give you something straight up. They always say you have to earn it.

As you pick up Mike's plate, you notice that he's arranged his mashed-up food into a smiley face. He's so gross.

After scraping the food into the compost bucket, you stack the dishes in the dishwasher. Then you take the bucket out into the backyard and dump it onto the compost pile. You do this every night. Ever since your parents decided to save their food scraps.

At first you thought they were really getting weird. Then they explained to you that food scraps can be recycled and turned into rich soil for the garden.

This all sounds good, but what it means to you right now is just one more thing you have to do. One more thing until you can call Kevin.

Thwop! The food scraps make a funny, wet sound as they slide out of the bucket into the pile. You hurry back and empty the garbage. And you're done!

"Mom? Dad?" No answer.

Better go to page 37.

"No! This isn't happening!" you shout, as you're lifted one more time and body-slammed to the parquet floor. And you're right—this shouldn't be happening. Billy is still across the room. Nobody is anywhere near you!

Groggily, you look over at Billy. He's staring with an intensity that could burn holes right through you.

His eyes shift upward. You feel your body move up off the floor with them. You hover in midair for a second. Then you spin upside down and crash to the floor one more time. But you don't feel it. The impact has knocked you out cold. It's as if you've been suspended in time and space. You feel nothing. You see nothing. It's simply the absence of everything.

Are you dead?

Find out on page 78.

16

SCREECH! The stepladder makes a horrible sound when you drag it over. You cringe.

"Shhh!" comes from a distant aisle.

Up the ladder. You can barely reach the top shelf. With your luck, you expect to come crashing down with all the books on top of you.

Fortunately, that doesn't happen. But there is a problem. You can't pull the phone book off the shelf. It's wedged in too tight. You struggle to pull it out. It takes both hands. You pull. Harder.

Whoosh! It comes free.

"Whoa!" You almost lose your balance. Slowly you climb down the stepladder. "They can put this phone book back themselves," you say under your breath. You're not about to climb back up there again.

Quickly you flip through the pages to Kevin's last name, Walker. You scan the list for his address. You never realized there would be so many Walkers. But there's nothing. No Walker with Kevin's address. You sigh in disgust and slam the book closed.

CRASH!

Find out what crashed on page 54.

Whoever it is sounds asthmatic. Then the person says something. It's hard to make out the words. It sounds like the person hasn't spoken in a long time.

"What?" you ask nervously.

The person repeats it.

The color drains from your face.

"Help me! Help me!" the voice croaks again.

"How? What?" you shout into the phone. *"Kevin? Is that you?"*

"I'm burning . . . I'm burn—" *Click.*

You slam the phone down, count to five, and hit redial.

Ring! Ring! Click.

The line is picked up. But this time it sounds different. There's an unfamiliar, crackling sound. At first it sounds like a roaring inferno. Then again, it could be . . .

Hurry to page 44.

18

"Dad!" you scream, reaching for the back of his head. The smell of burning hair is suffocating. You turn to Billy for help, but he's just sitting there, snickering at you and your dad.

Meanwhile, your dad tries to roll his head against the front seat of the car to put out the fire.

Not a good idea! Before he can lift his head back up, the car lurches forward. It veers off the road, rolls down an embankment, and comes to rest upside down at the bottom of a culvert.

Dazed, you realize you're pinned behind the front seat. You wonder if your dad and Billy are okay.

Then you hear something. *Click.* It's as if someone has just unbuckled his seat belt.

"Help me," you croak.

No answer. You hear a sliding sound. From the corner of your eye you see Billy crawling out of the wrecked car.

"Help me," you plead.

Find out if he will on page 72.

"Where's he going to go?" your dad asks as he puts the car in gear. "We'll be there in plenty of time."

The car ride is uneventful. The only problem is that you have to listen to your dad's favorite country-and-western station.

As you approach the airport, the traffic gets heavy. Cars are lined up for about a mile before the exit. You drum your fingers on the dash impatiently as the car inches forward.

"Come on," you whisper under your breath.

"Don't worry," your dad answers. "We'll get there."

As you round the curve of the exit, the airport comes into sight.

"Oh my gosh!" your dad gasps.

You look up. You can't believe it!

Go to page 53, now!

"Bogman!" you scream.

Bogman looks up at you with an evil smile. Your flesh is dripping from his mouth. He shakes his head. "Not Bogman. Billy. I'm your pen pal, Billy."

He holds his hand out as if he wants to shake yours.

Too stunned to realize what is happening, you reach up to shake his. Billy grabs your hand quickly and bites off a finger.

"Ahhhhhhhh!" you howl.

You're being eaten alive! You squirm to get away.

Suddenly you're falling . . . falling . . .

Thump!

Your head slams hard against something. It feels as if your brain has been crushed. Dizzily you open your eyes.

"Help!" you scream.

Turn to page 69.

22

You open the back door and get out. The ugly van driver steps back as you approach, letting go of your dad's shirt. "Hey, man, I'm sorry. Look, I don't want to fight. I just want to get home."

"Us too," your dad says calmly, adjusting his collar. "Give me your insurance information and let's be on our way."

The driver writes down the information.

"Thanks," your dad says as he takes the piece of paper.

You get back in and shut the car door. Billy hasn't said a word. Instead, his head is buried in a book. You think it's pretty weird for him to be reading when some guy is about to bust your dad in the nose. Curiously, you twist your head to see the title.

TELEKINESIS:
A 12-Step Program to Moving Matter

"What's that?" you ask.

Billy doesn't respond right away. He's staring straight ahead. Suddenly your dad slams on the brakes.

You gasp.

Find out why on page 29.

Until the last night of Billy's visit.

Your family and Billy are sitting down for a good-bye supper. It's your favorite: spaghetti and meatballs, and garlic bread. There's salad, too, but you know how to avoid that obstacle.

Once everyone is served, Billy gives you a devilish grin. He's up to something, but you're not sure what.

It doesn't take you long to figure it out. Tele-kinetically, Billy lifts a meatball off Mike's plate and drops it into his lap.

"Oops," your brother says as he scoops the meatball back onto his plate and wipes the sauce off his jeans.

You snicker and try to do Billy one better. Concentrating on your brother's water glass, you force it to tip over into his plate. Now Mike has spaghetti and meatball soup.

You and Billy almost fall out of your seats laughing. After a couple more tricks like this, you're bored and want to do something more exciting. But what?

Turn to page 85.

24

Until you find out how Billy's visit with Kevin went, you decide to postpone his visit with you. You figure if you send a letter tomorrow morning he'll get it this week. Plenty of time for him to cancel his plane reservations. All you have to do is think of a good lie.

Dear Billy,
Sorry, but I've got to cancel out on the visit.
My crazy aunt Jane is coming up for an operation, so my mom and dad said now is not a good time. Maybe next year we can get together.
Write back soon.
Me

Billy's reply doesn't take long. In fact, it takes such a short time that it makes you suspicious. A letter from Billy arrives in four days—a record time!

You nervously rip open the envelope and slide the letter out.

Read it on page 62.

Billy, however, just gives your dad a menacing look. Then he pulls the chandelier down on your dad's head.

Somehow, the table flying in your face makes you come to your senses. "Cover Billy's eyes!" you scream.

Quickly, your mom wraps her napkin around Billy's face while Mike pins Billy's arms behind him.

Suddenly you realize just what's been happening this week. The telekinesis technique hasn't just let you move things with your mind—it has changed your mind for the worse. You've become a selfish, egotistical maniac! You're lucky, however, because you were able to stop. You haven't been doing it long enough for it to completely take you over.

Billy, on the other hand, has gone completely off the deep end. All your parents can do is call the hospital. The doctors there tell you Billy is in for a long, tedious deprogramming treatment.

Now, every time you think of this visit with your pen pal, you breathe a sigh of relief. You never thought the mind could be so powerful.

The End

"A mons? What's a mons?" you mumble absentmindedly. Then you realize the word must have been MONSTER! Your jaw drops, but you recover quickly. Someone's playing a joke on you.

You pick up the envelope to look at the postmark. The name of the place where the letter came from is unreadable. You can only read the date. August 16! That was seven months ago!

"I'm going to kill you, Mike!"

"Whoa!" Mike yells with his hands up as you barge into his room. "I didn't do anything."

"Don't try to talk your way out of this one," you say. You wave the letter in his face. "You've kept this letter from me for seven months!"

"Wait," Mike says, backing away. "The letter came yesterday. I swear."

You look down at the envelope again. "But the postmark says August sixteenth!"

"It must've gotten lost in the mail," Mike says, shrugging.

You hesitate, not sure whether to believe him or not. He's done some pretty mean things to you.

"I swear," Mike repeats.

Turn to page 75.

You grab the first letter you see from Sue. She has her own stationery, with her name, address, and phone number printed on it in purple ink.

You run to use the phone in your parents' bedroom. You're kind of nervous. You've never spoken to Sue before.

"Hello?" says a soft, quiet voice.

"May I please speak to Sue?" you ask.

"Speaking."

You tell Sue who you are. "Billy's coming during spring vacation, but I think there's a problem," you say breathlessly.

"Spring vacation?" Sue says. "That's when—"

The line goes dead. You panic. Your heart races. "Sue!" you scream.

You stare at the phone in shock. Your hand is tightly wrapped around the cord. Then you see what happened.

Dangling from your fist is the plug at the end of the cord. You've ripped the cord out of the phone.

Exasperated, you dial Sue's number again.

Turn to page 52.

28

Your sneakers squeak as you cross the wide expanse of marble. Several pairs of eyes turn toward you. Someone whispers, "Shhh!"

As you reach the beginning of the third aisle to the left, you gulp. Huge wooden bookshelves tower over you, reaching almost to the ceiling. You peer down the aisle. The ancient shelves are leaning in. The thousands of books crammed on the shelves look as if they're about to fall off.

You scan the shelves. There are literally hundreds of phone books. You even see some in other languages. They're all in alphabetical order. Kansas City. Kauai. Kearny. Keene. Kellogg. Kenmore. Kenosha.

There it is! But just your luck. It's on the top shelf. You're going to have to use the stepladder.

Turn to page 16.

The van that hit your car has just exploded about a hundred feet down the road!

Your dad swerves around the ball of fire that used to be the van. By now the driver must be burned toast.

"Shouldn't we stop?" you cry.

Your dad hesitates. Then he spots a police cruiser speeding over. "I think they've got it under control. I'm ready to go home."

"Good idea," Billy seconds.

This reminds you to ask about the book again. But Billy gives you a look that says, *You're making me angry with that question.*

You look out the window, away from him.

The first thing you do when you walk in the house is open the dictionary.

tele-ki-ne-sis, n. The purported ability to move or deform inanimate objects through mental processes.

"What are inanimate objects?" you say out loud. You feel a hand on your back. You almost jump out of your skin.

Hurry to page 49.

30

"Sue?" you yell. "Sue? Are you still there?"

"Yes!" Sue answers. "And don't yell. I can hear you fine."

BLEEEEEEEP! The sound repeats itself. This time, however, the noise sounds familiar. You tell Sue to hold on. Then you set the phone down on the bed and dash downstairs.

Your brother, Mike, is standing on a chair in the kitchen. He's holding the phone up to the smoke detector and pushing the test button.

BLEEEEEEEP!

Mike is laughing so hard he's about to fall off the chair.

"Hey!" you scream.

Startled, Mike does lose his balance and fall. You grab the phone out of his hand and hang it up.

"I'm going to tell Mom!" you shout.

A devious smile cracks across his face. "Go ahead. Then I'll have to tell her you were making a long-distance call."

You storm out of the kitchen and back up to your parents' bedroom. "Listen, Sue," you say when you pick up the phone, "I've got to go. What should we do?"

Decide on page 84.

32

You tell your mom you'll give up baseball. You are so excited about Billy coming, though, that it's hard to feel disappointed.

Today is the day Billy arrives. All right! You have big expectations about his visit.

You and your mom drive to the airport to pick him up.

"Can you wait in the car?" you ask as your mom pulls up to the arrival gate. "I'm old enough to go in alone. Please?"

"Okay," she says reluctantly. "But don't fool around."

"I won't," you say, bounding out of the car just as your mom is turning on an oldies rock station.

You stop underneath a monitor displaying arrival gates and scan the list of arrivals. Billy's plane is arriving in ten minutes at gate 3. You're relieved because gate 3 is just a little way down the hall.

From the giant glass window at gate 3 you can see Billy's plane taxiing toward you.

You see a boy on board looking out a window over the wing. Billy? You're getting really excited.

Hurry to page 55.

You grab Billy by the shirt. He has jumped on the van driver's back. His arms are wrapped around the man's neck.

"Let's go, Billy," you plead. "My dad's taken care of it." To your astonishment, Billy slugs the van driver in the stomach!

You quickly climb back into the car. Billy is right behind you.

"Don't worry," your dad says. "I got his license plate number." He drives out the exit ramp and onto the highway.

"Is it going to cost a lot to fix?" you ask.

"I'll get the guy's money!" Billy yells. You gasp as he flings open the door while the car is moving.

"SHUT THAT DOOR NOW!" your dad orders.

Billy closes the door and glares at your dad through the rearview mirror. He's giving your dad such a killer look that you get nervous. You have a strange feeling that something's not right with Billy.

There's a fast-food restaurant up ahead. Maybe you should change the mood by suggesting a stop for milk shakes.

If you go for shakes, turn to page 59.

If you decide to let things ride, go to page 34.

You try to lighten the mood by telling a joke. It goes over like a lead balloon. Billy gives a little laugh. Then he cracks open his suitcase and pulls out a book.

"What're you reading?" you ask.

"None of your business," Billy answers. He turns his back to you so you can't see the book.

You slump in your seat. Your dad catches your eye in the rearview mirror. He raises his eyebrows. You make a face back. All you can think about is that this visit is starting out on the wrong foot. You crack open the soda Billy gave you and sip.

After a while you notice Billy staring at the back of your dad's head.

Absentmindedly, your dad rubs the spot. "Is it getting hot in here?" he asks.

"No," you answer.

"Well, I'm going to roll down the window," he says. You watch him swipe the back of his head again. But when his hand moves away, his hair is in flames!

Turn to page 18.

"Mom!" you shout at the top of your voice, without getting up from your bed or opening the door to your room.

No answer.

Maybe it's not such a good idea to shout. You don't want her angry when you talk to her. You jog downstairs and poke your head into the living room. "Mom?" you say sweetly.

Your mom looks up from her puzzle and raises her eyebrows.

"Mom," you repeat, then add "I've got a weird feeling about Billy's visit."

"Why?" your mom asks. "I thought you were excited about him coming."

You slump onto the couch. "I don't know. I just think it's strange that Kevin hasn't written me since Billy visited him. And there's something else." You fish the mysterious letter out of your pocket and hand it to your mom.

She adjusts her glasses and scans the letter. "This *is* strange. Billy is a monster?"

"That's what it says," you say, feeling kind of foolish. "What should I do?"

Turn to page 67.

36

"Let's try to find a parking space, Dad," you suggest. After you do, you head inside. The place is teeming with people.

You glance up at the arrival and departure screens and see "delayed" or "canceled" flashing on every flight listed, except . . .

Flight 781, Pensacola FL   *On Time*

"He's here," your dad calls. "Gate three."

You tuck yourself in tightly behind him and follow him to the security checkpoint. A huge crowd of people is pushing to get through, while security officers try to direct people away.

A large officer with a baton held high over his head speaks in a loud voice. "Please, go to the waiting area for an update. Gates three through seventeen are temporarily closed."

Your dad elbows his way up to another officer. "We've got a young boy we're supposed to meet at gate three. What's going on?"

"Turbulence," the officer responds. "There are gale-force winds over the airport. No planes can land."

Turn to page 80.

You dash through the house. They're in the living room. Your dad is reading the newspaper. Your mom is at a card table working on a puzzle with a zillion pieces.

"I'm done cleaning up. Can I call Kevin now?" you ask.

"Yes," your mom says.

In the kitchen you dig into your pocket for Kevin's phone number, but you come up empty.

"What?" you say. Frantically, you search all your pockets. Nothing. They're all empty.

You run upstairs to your room and dig through the mess on your desk and the pile of clothes on your floor. Still nothing.

You go into the dining room and search under the table. Your hand lands on something. A slimy piece of eggplant. Yuck!

After you wash your hands, you check out the silverware drawer. The refrigerator. The dishwasher. The kitchen cabinets.

No luck.

"It has to be somewhere," you say anxiously. Then you get a brainstorm. There's one place you haven't looked. But do you have to?

Do it on page 45.

This is exciting! You can just imagine all the tricks you can learn to play on your brother . . . at school . . . everywhere!

"I guess," Billy answers. "But you have to promise not to tell anyone else about it." He pulls the telekinesis book out of his suitcase. He takes you through each step of the process.

The first time you try it, nothing happens. For two days you get no results, but by the end of the week you're lifting pencils, erasers, cups, and other small objects a foot off the ground.

The power you feel is incredible. It's like nothing you've ever felt before. For the first time in your life you're not afraid of Mike pounding you. You know you can handle yourself under any circumstances. You can just move things or people until you have them where you want them.

At the same time, you and Billy are having the best week ever. You never expected to have so much fun.

UNTIL . . .

Find out on page 23.

You turn around. Standing before you is a small, skinny, brown-haired boy wearing a torn pair of jeans and a red T-shirt. He grins.

"Billy?" you say in astonishment.

"Hey, can I have a bowl of cereal, too?" Billy asks. "I'm starving."

"B-But you're not supposed to be here until this afternoon," you stammer.

"I know," Billy says, "but I caught an earlier flight and took a cab here. I just couldn't wait any longer." He spreads his hands. "And after all, I did know the address, pen pal!" He slugs you in the shoulder.

You can't believe he took a cab by himself. "How'd you get in?" you ask.

"The back door was unlocked," Billy tells you. He looks around the kitchen. "Cool house!"

This isn't making any sense. Your mom checks every lock in the house before she goes to bed. You realize Mike must have left the door unlocked. He does that sometimes.

"Well, uh, what kind of cereal do you want?" you ask.

Turn to page 82.

Billy tosses you down the baggage ramp. You tumble head over heels down a thirty-foot drop. Luckily you land on a pile of soft luggage with only a few bumps and bruises.

Up above, Billy has already walked away from the baggage pickup area.

But you don't see this. You are struggling to get to your feet. Suddenly a heavy suitcase crashes on your head.

You pass out and are carted away to the lost-baggage room. Above you, Billy glances around the terminal. A wide, toothy grin spreads across his face. It is not a friendly grin. The gleam in his eyes is cold, heartless . . . *evil!*

Billy picks up an old, beat-up suitcase on the baggage carousel and walks to the other side of the airport. He climbs the stairs to the terminal, reaches into his pocket, and pulls out an airline ticket. On it is stamped a flight number and a departure time of ten minutes from now. The destination is . . .

Abilene, Texas.

The End

42

You drop the suitcase. Immediately the invisible hand lets go of your throat. You stumble into the hallway and collapse, coughing.

Billy brushes the hair out of your face. "Are you all right?" he asks, sounding very concerned.

"Not really," you spit out. "You almost killed me!"

"Me? What did I do?" Billy asks. "I was standing here and suddenly you're on the floor, choking. It must have been something you ate."

"N-No," you sputter nervously. You inch away from Billy.

Billy stands up. "I'll get you a glass of water," he says.

Just then, you hear your dad's heavy, thudding footsteps. "What's going on down here?" he asks, storming into the room. "Are you sick?"

You shake your head. You're trying to find the words to explain what happened when Billy comes into the hallway with a glass of water.

"Who are you?" your dad asks.

Go to page 50.

You're sure Kevin gave you his phone number in one of his early letters. You dive into the pile to find it. Dozens of letters scatter across your bedspread. Lots of them are from Kevin. You can't believe how many letters he wrote. It only confirms your feeling that something must be wrong. You wonder if you wrote something rude. You don't think so, but you can't be sure.

Luckily, there are postmarks with dates on every envelope. This helps you sort through the stack faster to get to the oldest ones.

But no luck. None of the letters you find has Kevin's phone number. You must have lost the one that did.

Quickly you pile the letters back in the box and shove it under your bed. You can't call information—you'd need to know the name of Kevin's parents, and you don't.

Now you're not sure what to do.

Keep looking for Kevin's number?
Hurry to page 10.

Call Sue and see if she's had any letters from Kevin? Check out page 27.

Or tell someone about your suspicions?
Go to page 57.

44

A bad connection.

A cold, tinny, recorded voice comes on the line. "The number you have dialed is not in service at this time. Please check your number and dial again."

You run back into the living room. "Something crazy just happened!"

Your dad looks over the top rim of his glasses at you. "What?"

You tell them.

"Someone's playing a trick," your mom says.

You shake your head, determined to convince them. "That's not it. I just know it."

Neither your dad nor your mom seems to be taking you seriously. "Maybe you dialed a wrong number," your dad suggests.

They're not paying attention to what you're saying at all. You stomp your foot. "No," you say. "Something's wrong. I know it." You leave, angry that you're not being listened to.

On the way up to your room, you think for the first time that maybe Billy shouldn't visit right now. Maybe you should clear up this Kevin mystery first.

If you want to bag Billy's visit, go to page 24.

If you feel like taking your chances with Billy, go to page 77.

The compost pile.

With a flashlight in one hand, you pick through the remains of tonight's supper. You use a stick to poke at the pile, pushing potatoes and salad aside.

It's disgusting. It's gross. You can't believe you're doing this. But you need to find Kevin's number now! You won't sleep tonight unless you do. You can't wait for tomorrow to go back to the library. And the last thing you want to do is climb back up that stepladder.

You pick through some more stinky garbage. A stained corner of paper shines under the flashlight's beam. Gingerly, you pull it out. It's Kevin's phone number!

Back in the kitchen, you carefully lay the slimy piece of paper on a napkin. You're afraid if you handle it too much, it'll fall apart.

You dial the number. It's ringing.

Click. Someone picks up.

"Hello," you say. "Is Kevin there?"

Silence. Someone is breathing on the other end. Rasping, as if they're having trouble catching their breath.

"Hello?" you repeat.

Turn to page 17.

46

The people in the terminal begin to cheer. A menacing smile, however, spreads across Billy's face. He walks over to the window.

You hear him mutter under his breath. "That's what they think. . . ."

You follow Billy over to the window and look up into the sky. An airplane is descending toward the runway. Suddenly the plane starts to vibrate violently.

Miraculously, the pilot is able to gain control and pull back up into the air before the plane crashes.

As you gasp, you can hear Billy laughing beside you.

"Nobody's landing at this airport as long as I'm here," Billy says angrily. "Not after how that stewardess treated me."

"What?" you answer, totally confused. "What can you do about it?"

"Anything I want," Billy sneers. *Whoosh!* All of a sudden you're swept off your feet. You begin to levitate a foot off the ground!

"Let me down!" you scream. "Dad, help!"

Billy looks away. You fall to the ground. When you get to your feet, he's gone.

Find out where on page 79.

Two days after you send a letter explaining to Billy why he can't come to visit, the doorbell rings. You're in the middle of your homework and are not thrilled that you've been interrupted. The doorbell rings repeatedly, as if the person outside is in a hurry.

"I'll get it!" you yell. You hope it's the mailman with the CDs you ordered from the music club. You swing open the door. It's not the mailman. It's not anyone you know. It's some small, brown-haired kid with a suitcase.

"We're not interested in buying anything," you say, starting to close the door. But before the latch slides home, the door bursts off its hinges and slams you to the floor.

You're dazed. Spots and stars dance before your eyes. Vaguely, you can hear shouting, but it takes you a minute to make out the words.

"What do you mean by dumping me?" the voice shouts. "Nobody turns me down, you little gnat! I'll crush you like a bug for treating me like that!"

"Who . . . Who are you?" you sputter, pushing the door off your chest.

Blink twice and go to page 9.

48

Hey, Pen Pal!
Guess what? Billy's coming to visit. I
can't wait. It's going to be so cool. We're
not going to get any sleep. My mom says
we can do anything we want. I want to
go to Lakeland and ride the roller
coaster until we barf! He'll be here
in one week. You probably won't
hear from either of us until afterward.
Hope you're jealous. Gotta go.
Kevin

You frown. You haven't heard from Kevin
since that letter. More than nine months ago! It
seems funny that he wouldn't write and tell
you about his time with Billy. Kevin would
write if his dog broke a toenail!

In fact, Kevin wrote more letters than you,
Sue, and Billy combined. Sometimes you even
wished he'd slow down, because you couldn't
keep up. Kevin was a letter-writing fool. And
he was a good writer, too.

Just then, another letter slips from the pile
onto the floor. You pick it up. It's from Sue. You
read it over. It's from last fall.

Turn to page 7.

It's just your mom, looking over your shoulder. You ask her what an inanimate object is.

"Anything that isn't alive. Like a chair, a car, or a house," she says.

"How can someone move things with their mind?" you ask.

"They can't," your mom answers. "It's just some trick magicians do to make you think they can move things without touching them."

"Oh," you say. "Well, Billy's reading a book on it."

As you say this, Billy comes banging through the front door. Your mom reaches out her hand and introduces herself. Billy shakes her hand and smiles sweetly.

"You can take your bag right upstairs to the left," your mom says, pointing to your room at the top of the stairs.

"Thanks!" Billy says, dashing up the stairs.

She turns to you. "What a nice boy."

You nod, but you're not so sure you agree. You run upstairs to see how Billy is settling in, in your room. On the way, however, a sudden chill runs down your spine.

What if . . .

Explore your suspicions on page 88.

50

"I'm Billy. I'm supposed to visit this week," Billy explains, handing you the glass.

Your dad looks confused. "What got you coughing so?"

"Well, uh . . . ," you begin to explain, nervously eyeing Billy.

But Billy interrupts you. "Choked on the prize in the cereal box," he says matter-of-factly.

You shoot him a puzzled look. Another set of footsteps comes down the stairs. It's your mom. Her hair is sticking straight up, and her eyes are bloodshot. As she walks into the kitchen, her mouth is stretched open in the widest yawn you've ever seen. Then she stops dead in her tracks.

"Who are you?" she asks, looking at Billy.

"That's Billy," your dad answers quickly.

Your mom shakes her head. "You're not supposed to be here until this afternoon."

"I caught an early flight," Billy explains.

Your mom looks at Billy suspiciously. She shrugs and then bends over to pick up Billy's suitcase.

"Uh, Mom . . . Mom . . . MOM!" you scream.

Flip to page 63.

52

Sue picks up on the first ring. "What happened?" She sounds worried.

"I accidentally hung up," you explain.

"Well, what I was trying to say is that Billy is supposed to visit *me* during spring break," she says in one big breath.

"What?" you say. "He's coming to my house on March twenty-second. The first Saturday of vacation."

"Billy's supposed to arrive at my house on the twenty-fourth," Sue says.

"No way! He said he's going to visit me for the entire week!"

"Hey, I don't know," Sue says. "Maybe he got mixed up."

"Have you heard from Kevin lately?" you ask.

"Nah," she says, "but I wouldn't worry about it. He always seemed kind of flaky to me. He probably just got tired of writing."

"I guess," you say, somewhat disappointed. "It's nice to finally speak to you."

"Yeah," Sue answers.

BLEEEEP! An incredibly loud sound interrupts your phone conversation.

What now? Flip to page 30.

The traffic entering the airport is beyond horrendous. Horns blare. People are out of their cars, yelling at each other. It's a total traffic jam. And it doesn't look as if it's going to be cleared up anytime soon.

You sink in your seat. "I can't believe this is happening to me," you complain.

"Don't worry, sport," your dad says cheerfully. "It'll break up in a minute."

You shake your head in complete disgust. You've lost all patience with your dad. You want to scream. But you don't because no one will hear you over the din of car horns blasting everywhere.

"Look, Dad," you say, turning to him. "I'm going to walk up to the terminal and see if I can find Billy."

Your dad shakes his head. "I don't want you wandering around the airport without me."

A pained expression appears on your face. You hate it when your dad treats you like a little kid. "I'm not a kid," you argue. But before you can say anything else, something at the front of the traffic jam catches your eye.

See it on page 86.

54

"Ouch!" you cry, rubbing your head.

A dozen phone books have slipped off the top shelf and landed squarely on your head. There was a real reason they were jammed in so tight.

You push the phone books aside. There's no way you're going to put all of them back.

You stand up. Out of the corner of your eye, you spy another phone book for Kenosha, Wisconsin.

"Huh?" You fish it out of the pile. It's last year's phone book. Figuring you have nothing to lose, you look up *Walker* at Kevin's address.

Bingo! It's there. You scribble the phone number on a piece of paper and hurry home.

Inside the house, you grab the kitchen phone. Your fingers fly over the number pad. *Ring!*

You smile. You're certain you're going to get to the bottom of this. You'll talk to Kevin and find out why he stopped writing. And it will have nothing to do with Billy's visit.

Nervously, you spin so your back is to the phone. Suddenly you hear a click. You've been disconnected. You hear . . . NOTHING!

Better go to page 83.

The arm of the exit ramp extends like an accordion to the plane's door.

You step away from the window to meet Billy as he exits. Twenty or so people hurry off the ramp. Then there's a pause. No one comes off for about thirty seconds. You know the plane must be packed. You can't understand why there would be a break in the crowd getting off.

Then you see a small, skinny, brown-haired boy run up the ramp. He's wearing a torn pair of jeans and a red T-shirt. He grins. You wave.

"Hi! I'm Billy!" he says when he reaches you. Then he grabs your arm and pulls. "Come on! Let's get out of here!"

Without thinking, you follow, but you look back when you hear yelling.

"Stop that kid!" a flight attendant yells.

You stop, thinking they mean you, but Billy tugs at your shirt. "Let's go!"

You point back toward Billy's plane. "But . . . I think they want something."

"Don't worry about them," Billy huffs. "I slammed the plane door in their face because they were rude to me. So now they're mad."

Turn to page 65.

56

Billy is right below it. The small turboprop flattens him on the tarmac like a squished bug.

It isn't until you've been questioned by the police for a grueling eight hours that you learn who Billy really is.

Apparently, Billy had paranormal abilities. He was able to move things telekinetically. And he was very good at it. The problem, however, was that his skill made him feel as though he were more powerful than anyone else on earth. When anyone made him angry, he went nuts.

What set him off this time was a stewardess giving him the wrong lunch. He wanted steak, and she gave him chicken. He hated chicken. And he felt justified in taking revenge on the entire airport for the stewardess's mistake. Except, in the end, the airport took its own revenge!

The End

This is creepy. You need to consult with someone who has more experience.

But who? Your teacher Mr. McGrew is cool. You can always talk to him. But it's Saturday. You'd have to wait until Monday.

Your dad is always ready to help, even though sometimes he's a total dork. But he's at work. He works Tuesday through Saturday at the bottling plant.

Hmmm. "Well, there's always Mom," you mutter without much enthusiasm. She's pretty good at helping you out with things. But she's such a mom. She can be really embarrassing.

What about your brother, Mike?

Choose on page 35.

58

"Why'd you grab the suitcase?" you ask.

Billy shrugs. He picks it up. "I like to carry my own stuff."

Playfully you snatch the suitcase back.

Billy's eyes flash with anger. He doesn't move a muscle. But somehow your fingers are pried loose!

"Cool!" you say as you innocently pick up the suitcase again. "How'd you do that?"

But your excitement quickly fades when you feel a hand wrapped around your throat. Fingers squeeze your larynx. Your eyes bug out. You try to talk. But you can't—because you're choking!

Gasp! Turn to page 42.

Billy inches toward your dad.

You lean against the front seat, separating them. "Let's stop for some milk shakes."

"Terrific idea," your dad says.

"I want chocolate," you say decisively. "What about you, Billy?"

Billy rubs his eyes as if he's breaking out of a trance. "Strawberry."

"I'm not sure they have strawberry," your dad says as you pull in the parking lot.

A flash of anger clouds Billy's face again.

"I want you to show me your curveball when we get to my house," you tell Billy after you get your shakes. They had strawberry.

Billy relaxes. "Sure." He smiles.

Whew, you tell yourself. Billy's a time bomb. I better not get him angry this week.

The rest of the day goes smoothly. No more accidents. No arguments. No nothing.

You keep Billy outside playing catch all afternoon, while your dad tells your mom about Billy's temper. You're worried that there might be trouble between Mike and Billy.

You're about to find out. Mike is walking toward the two of you.

Flip to page 74.

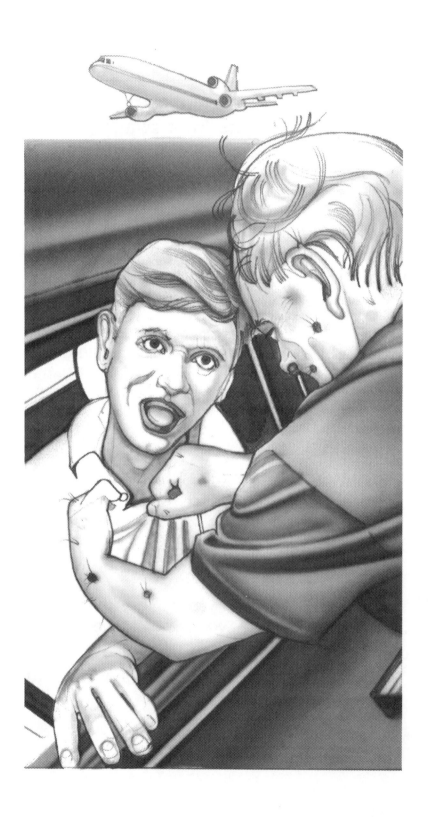

"Thanks," you say excitedly as you take the can. You barely notice the dozen or so people on foot racing past your car. The traffic jam is beginning to move. Your car inches forward.

SCREECH! The sound of crumpling metal drowns you out. Your head snaps backward.

The van behind you has just smashed into the rear of your car.

"Hey!" your dad yells. Then he turns back to you. "Are you two all right?"

You nod and look at Billy.

"I think so," Billy says, rubbing his neck.

Suddenly the ugliest man you've ever seen pokes his face through the window. "Why don't you drive! This isn't a parking lot. This is a road."

Startled, your dad reels backs. The face belongs to the driver of the van that hit you. His skin is blotchy red, with black hairs growing out of the strangest places. To your horror, the van driver grabs your dad's shirt collar.

What should you do?

If you think you should go for help, turn to page 6.

If you confront the guy, turn to page 22.

62

Hey, Pen Pal,
Don't sweat it. Sue's invited me to her
house for spring break. We'll do it next
year. I'll write again next week.
Billy

It's as if a giant weight is lifted from your shoulders. For a minute, you worry about Sue's safety. But you're probably just being silly. If Sue thought something strange was going on, she would have written you about it.

To your surprise, you don't get a letter from Sue this week. You fire off a letter to her, asking how Billy's visit went. But no reply comes.

You write to Billy. But he doesn't answer you, either. You start to worry. You stop writing.

Three months go by. Your mom and dad occasionally ask you why you have stopped writing to your pen pals. You always give an evasive answer. How can you explain without sounding like a nutcase?

That is, until one morning at breakfast when you get up from the table to refill your glass of OJ and inadvertently glance over your dad's shoulder at his newspaper.

Uh-oh! Go to page 87 now!

The suitcase flies out of her hands. Your mom reels backward as if she's been punched. But nobody has swung a fist.

Your dad moves toward your mom to help her, but then he doubles over, just as though he's been punched in the stomach.

Before anyone can react, Billy grabs the suitcase and dashes down the hall. With a loud boom, he smashes through the front door without even opening it.

Your mom sits on the floor, dazed, trying to speak. "Call the police."

Your dad stumbles over to the phone and dials 911. It doesn't take more than a few minutes for two police officers to enter the kitchen and take your statements. They call in over their walkie-talkies.

Within minutes, a crackling is heard over one officer's radio. Several numbers are repeated. They make no sense to you. But the officers seem to understand the code, and they dash from the kitchen.

Hurry to page 5.

64

A photo of Billy is splashed across the television screen. The announcer reports, "A young maniac is loose in the city. Earlier today a brown-haired boy escaped with the help of accomplices in a green, four-door sedan."

That's your car!

The screen shows the ugly van driver standing next to a reporter. He's got a black eye where Billy punched him. The reporter sticks the mike in his face.

"They almost killed me trying to escape!" the van driver says.

You look over at Billy. He has slipped out of your dad's grasp. You leap and tackle him before he can take a step. Then you and your dad lock Billy in a closet while your mom calls the police.

At the hospital, while Mike gets his arm set, you and your mom sit in the waiting room. Your dad is off by the elevators talking to a police officer.

Finally your dad comes over. He shrugs. "What a nutty kid. I wish we had known."

"What d'ya mean?" you ask.

Find out on page 73.

"You shouldn't have done that," you protest mildly.

Billy gives you a deadly look. You follow, not knowing what else to do.

As the two of you walk through the terminal, you notice Billy moving his head back and forth, as if he's looking for something. Every few feet you see someone trip and fall unexpectedly. Each time it happens, Billy nearly doubles over with laughter. You, on the other hand, are feeling increasingly nervous about the way Billy is acting. He seems pretty mean.

At the baggage pickup you try to find out what happened on the plane, but Billy ignores you.

"Really, what happened?" you persist.

Billy grabs the front of your shirt in his fist. "Listen," he says angrily, "if you're going to be such a pain, why don't you go home to Mama, little baby?"

You're stunned. You never expected Billy to be so mean! "You can't treat people like this," you protest.

"Oh, no?" Billy says. His eyes take on an evil gleam. "Well, try this."

Find out what happens on page 41.

66

Now, however, the idea of Kevin vanishing and not reappearing just doesn't sit right. In fact, the more you think about it, the weirder it seems. Kevin would never just *stop*. He'd write a million letters explaining *why* he was stopping. Something's not right. And you could kick yourself for not thinking about it until now! Just when you open a letter accusing Billy of being a monster. You can't help thinking that if Billy really *is* a monster, that might be why Kevin stopped writing. Maybe Billy did something to him.

Your breath shortens, and your heart begins to race at this thought. You make up your mind. You *have* to call Kevin and find out why he stopped writing.

Turn to page 43.

"One of your pen pal friends is playing a joke," your mom says emphatically. "But it's up to you. If you want to call his visit off, just say so." She hands the letter back.

You think hard. Sue is a real prankster. It must be from her. There's no reason not to have Billy visit.

You nod as you make your decision. "Billy is coming."

Your mom pats your hand. "Good. I'm glad."

Finally, the day of Billy's arrival comes. You wake before dawn and pull on your favorite jeans and T-shirt. Quietly you slip through the dark house to the kitchen and pour yourself a big bowl of cereal.

Billy isn't arriving until this afternoon. You're planning to clean your room and get it ready for him this morning. It won't be easy. There are piles of junk under your bed, in your closet, and just about everywhere.

You lean over your cereal bowl and try to formulate a plan for attacking your room. Then you hear a cough. Right behind you!

Better go to page 39.

You decide to ignore Mike. As usual, he has nothing to tell you.

Finally it's the day of Billy's arrival.

"Come on, Dad," you plead. Billy's plane lands in an hour. If you don't leave now, you'll be late. Your dad, however, is dawdling over the thousand-piece puzzle on the card table.

"Just a sec," he says. He waves a hand distractedly at you. "There's just twenty pieces left. I want to finish this before we leave."

You slump against the door frame and groan. "What's left to do?"

"Just the sky," he says.

Great, you think. The sky is all one color. It could take him hours trying to fit those last pieces together. "Come on, Dad," you whine.

"Go out to the car. I'll be there in a minute," he tells you.

You shrug and leave. In the car you wait another fifteen minutes before he comes jogging out.

"Finished it!" he says proudly. "See what a little persistence will do?"

You sigh. "We're going to miss Billy."

Turn to page 19.

Your mom runs into your room, followed by your dad. "What's the matter, hon?" she asks sleepily.

"I . . . I was being eaten alive!"

"Don't be silly," your dad says with a laugh.

"But my leg," you plead. "Look at my leg! And my hand! One of my fingers is gone!"

"No," your mom says soothingly. Her fingers brush your cheek. "It was a bad dream." She lays her hand on your brow. "You have a fever. And your eyes are red." She frowns. "I hope you don't have pinkeye. We'd better go see Dr. Turiansky tomorrow."

You try to sit up, but you're too disoriented.

"But . . . but Billy was . . ." You stop yourself. Your parents won't understand. Your dad picks you up and puts you back in bed. Your mom tucks the blankets around you, turns out the light, and closes the door.

As you drift back to sleep, you decide that Billy is definitely not coming for a visit. Not ever.

The End

70

Anxiously you cross the hall to your room. You look around for Billy's book, but you don't see it. "Where's that cool book you were reading?" you ask.

Billy shrugs. "Wanna play some ball?"

"Yeah, sure," you answer. "But I'd rather know about this telekinesis stuff. Can you really do it?"

There's a long silence. Billy seems reluctant to tell you anything.

Nevertheless, you're persistent. "Spill the beans. What are you doing with a book on telekinesis?" you ask.

Billy looks down at his feet. "Just having a little fun."

"Like what?" you respond. "Can you bend spoons?"

"Well, sort of," Billy begins. "I've never really tried to bend spoons, but I've moved other things. Watch."

Billy stares at the chair across the room. It levitates on its own.

"Cool!" you say. "Can I learn?"

Find out if you can on page 38.

Billy doesn't even look at you. You see his feet as he stands by the upside-down car. He kneels down and reaches his arm through the shattered window.

He's going to help you. Or is he?

Billy snakes his hand around the crushed door frame. You hear him grunt as he strains to reach into the car.

"Help me," you plead one more time.

Billy looks across the car at you. Your eyes meet. He hesitates, but only for a second. He reaches for the book he was reading. Then you black out.

Two days later, you wake up in the hospital.

"Where's Billy?" you mumble.

Your mother covers your face with kisses. "Oh, honey, you're talking!" she exclaims. Then she frowns. "Billy disappeared. Nobody has seen him since the accident."

"Is Dad okay?" you ask.

Your mom nods. Relief shows on her face. "You're both going to recover fully."

The End

Your dad shakes his head. "According to the officer, Billy slashed the tires of most of the cars at the airport. That's why there was a traffic jam when we picked him up."

You put your face in your hands. "What luck," you say to your parents. "I have to be pen pals with a criminal."

"Not just a criminal," your dad adds, "but a psycho. He also burned down his parents' house—with them in it!"

The End

74

"Hey, dweebs. Playing patty-cake?"

You ignore Mike. From long experience you know that this is the best strategy.

"Who's your friend?" Mike asks.

"This is Billy," you answer, hoping that Mike will just go away.

"Well, hey, Billy," Mike says with a big grin. He reaches out a hand to shake.

When Billy reciprocates, Mike grabs Billy's hand and flips him with a judo move your dad taught him.

You expect Billy to be lying flat on the ground with the wind knocked out of him, but instead he's back on his feet in a flash. Then he lunges at Mike.

Mike, however, steps to the side, and Billy falls on his face in the grass. When Billy rolls over, you can tell he's not amused.

A sneer spreads across his face. You can hear a strange gurgling in his throat. He clamps his jaw down and stares menacingly at Mike.

Suddenly you hear a nasty, bone-shattering crack. Mike screams bloody murder. He falls to the ground, writhing, with one of his arms twisted oddly behind him.

Hurry to page 13.

"You'd better be telling the truth," you say, stalking back into your room. You dump the contents of a plastic storage box on your bed. About two hundred letters fall out. You and Billy have been writing each other for two years. You're part of a pen pal chain of four kids: Billy in Florida, Kevin in Wisconsin, Sue in Texas, and you. Once a month you write letters.

You sort through the letter pile, stopping to read one from Billy. It's about baseball. He's a pitcher, like you. Only your record is better than his. You're psyched for him to show you his wicked curveball.

"I can't wait to meet you," you say, grinning at the letter.

Then your eye catches the edge of another envelope, postmarked Kenosha, Wisconsin. It's a letter from Kevin. Come to think of it, he hasn't written to you in a while. You fish the letter out of the envelope and lay it flat on your lap.

Go to page 48.

76

"I don't want to hear it," she says. "You have a choice. You can either tell Billy he can't come for spring break because you broke a family rule, or you can skip baseball this year."

Your face blanches. You can't believe you're getting such a severe punishment. What's going on?

Has your mom flipped her wig? Is she nuts? "It was just a phone call," you plead.

"I don't care," your mom answers. "It's about time you learned to follow rules."

Oh, no! She's using the phone call as an example. You hate it when she wants you to learn a lesson. It always means you're beat.

If you decide to skip baseball, go to page 32.

If you bag Billy's visit, go to page 47.

You go upstairs to bed, but you can't sleep. You open the latest Bogman comic book. Bogman is an ancient Celtic warrior who was buried nearly two thousand years ago in a bog in western Ireland. Lightning struck and brought him back to life. Now he roams the world in search of his lost love, Gweyn. In this issue demons try to enlist Bogman in an army of ghouls to take over the world. It's a classic battle between good and evil.

At first, Bogman seems to be drawn to the demons. He's been put in a trance, and he goes about the land wreaking havoc. . . .

Suddenly you hear the doorbell ring. You hop up and stare out your bedroom window into the dark night. Who could it be?

You open your bedroom door and creep downstairs. Everyone is asleep. You guess no one else heard the bell. You turn on the porch light and unlock the door.

You hesitate before opening the door. The doorbell rings again, this time more insistently.

"Keep your shirt on!" you say.

The door swings wide open. Something grabs your arm—and begins to chew!

Hurry to page 21.

78

Luckily, you're not dead. You just have a broken arm, collarbone, and leg. You've also cracked your skull and have an awful concussion.

You wake up in the hospital. Your mom and dad are hovering over you.

When your parents see you open your eyes, they rush to speak. "You were beaten pretty badly," your mom says worriedly. "Who did this to you?"

You moan. How can you explain? It was more like a dream than something real. No one touched you. Billy was there, but he didn't lift a finger.

"Where's Billy?" you croak.

"Billy who?" your dad asks.

You start to speak again, but you don't. You realize that there's no way you can explain this without sounding completely nuts.

The End

"What's up, sport?" your dad asks, coming over.

You point toward the sky, but your dad doesn't understand. "It's Billy," you say. "He's not human." Then you spot Billy out on the tarmac. His arms are raised.

Your dad sees him, too. "He's going to get hurt down there!" He runs over to the check-in counter to call for help.

You press your hands against the window and watch. It's as if Billy really *is* in control of the universe. All the planes are circling around him. Then he begins to spin a small, empty turboprop in the air. It spins and spins. Faster and faster. But suddenly Billy seems to lose control of it. The plane drops like a lead sinker. Unfortunately . . .

Turn to page 56.

80

A screech sounds from a walkie-talkie just around the corner. Then you hear, "Copy, O'Reilly. Hold on."

"Roger, central," a voice says into it. You hear a laugh that doesn't sound like an adult's. You poke your head around the corner and see a small, brown-haired boy holding a walkie-talkie close to his mouth. He speaks into it. "Control, we've got an eight-six-eight-six over on the west tarmac. Please send immediate assistance."

"What's an eight-six-eight-six?" you ask innocently.

The boy looks up. He smiles and shrugs. "Who knows? I just found this and decided to fool around with it."

You're jolted by a bolt of recognition. It's Billy! He looks just like the photograph he sent you.

You start to talk, but the public address system interrupts you. "Attention, passengers! Attention, passengers! All flights are now back on schedule. The gale-force winds have stopped."

Hurry to page 46.

"Whatever you're having," Billy answers easily. He plops down on the chair beside you.

You set him up with a bowl and spoon and watch as he pours his cereal and milk. "My favorite!"

After a few awkward moments, you feel like you've known Billy forever. You and he talk about what you want to do this week.

"My dad is going to take us to a major-league baseball game," you tell him excitedly. "And we're going to go to Wild Times—it's a really cool amusement park. There's an awesome roller coaster there." You talk nonstop. By the time you finish telling Billy all your plans, your fears about him being a monster are completely forgotten.

Since you've finished your cereal, you grab Billy's suitcase. "Let's go up to my room!" You start down the hallway, expecting Billy to be right at your heels.

Suddenly Billy grabs the suitcase, ripping it out of your hand.

You spin around. Billy is still sitting at the table, the suitcase at his feet!

Hurry to page 58.

You spin around.

Your mom's finger is resting on the phone. She looks angry.

"Who said you could make a long-distance call?" she asks.

"Uh . . . uh . . . I was just . . ." How did she know? She must have heard you dial a long string of numbers.

"You were just what?" she snaps. "Who do you need to call long-distance? And in the middle of the day! Do you know what a call this time of day costs?"

"Uh, no," you answer meekly.

"Your father and I are not made of money," your mom says. She drums her fingers on the kitchen countertop.

"But you don't understand. I need to call Kevin," you beg. "Billy visited him last summer, and I haven't heard from Kevin since."

Your mom sticks her hand out. You drop the receiver into it. "Kevin probably got tired of writing," she says.

"I know, but . . ."

"Don't *I know, but* me," your mom says testily. "I'll think about letting you call."

Turn to page 4.

"I'll write Billy and tell him he's a doofus for scheduling two trips at the same time," Sue answers.

"Good idea," you say. You hear heavy footsteps on the stairs. And they're not your brother's. "Gotta go!"

Click. You hang up.

And just in time.

"What are you doing?" your mom says angrily as she bursts into the room.

Panicking, you try to hide the phone. "Nothing," you answer. The phone crashes to the floor.

"Uh-huh," your mom says with satisfaction. "Nothing? Well, pick up that nothing and put it back on my nightstand."

"Sure, Mom," you say compliantly.

"Who were you calling?"

"My pen pal. Not Billy. Sue, in Abilene, Texas. I know I'm not supposed to make long-distance calls without your approval, but this was—" You stop midsentence. Your mom is holding her hand up.

Turn to page 76.

You decide it's time for Billy and you to go head-to-head. You want to prove that you can top Billy in anything. And you feel confident that you can. In fact, you feel so confident, you don't think anyone can compete against you. This telekinetic technique has made you feel as if you have superhuman powers. No one can beat you.

With this in mind, you flip Billy's spoon down his shirt.

Surprised, Billy retaliates by stuffing your napkin into your mouth.

You try to do one better by stuffing the edge of the tablecloth into his mouth.

Next, Billy lifts the entire table and uses it to smash you against the wall. "Nobody can beat me," he laughs, completely out of control.

Your parents jump up, horrified. "Stop that now!" your dad shouts.

Turn to page 25.

A humongous crowd of people is chasing someone. You try to get a glimpse of who it is, but you can't see over the roofs of the cars. All you see are dozens of heads bobbing as they snake through the cars.

Quickly you open your door and climb up onto the roof of the car.

In the distance you see a small boy with brown hair, about thirty feet in front of the pack. For some unknown reason, you get a sinking feeling in your stomach. That kid looks just like . . . just like . . .

Go after the kid on page 8.

Stay in the car and wait until you can park on page 36.

ABILENE ARSON STILL UNSOLVED!

Abilene, TX

Authorities have not given up hope in the tragic "Abilene Arson" case, a mystery that has stumped authorities for over three months. The Marchant family—Rob Marchant, his wife, Sally, and daughter, Sue—disappeared after their home burned to the ground under mysterious circumstances three months ago. Anyone with information as to their location, please contact the Abilene Police Department. . . .

Slowly you sink into your chair. "Oh, no!"

"What?" Your dad looks at you curiously.

"Nothing." You shake your head. You can't tell your dad. He'll think you're crazy. So you bite your tongue. All you can do is thank your lucky stars that Billy didn't come to visit you.

The End

88

What if Billy can perform telekinesis? What if that guy's van didn't explode by itself—what if Billy *made* it explode?

Nah! You shake your head in disbelief. "That's crazy," you mutter.

Or is it? The thought nags at you even though you know it's ludicrous. Your teachers always said you had a vivid imagination.

Just then the singsong voice of your older brother, Mike, echoes in your mind. You play back your memory of Mike taunting you about having a letter about Billy.

In a flash you're in Mike's bedroom, rifling his drawers. It's not there. And you've checked all his secret hiding places.

Turn to page 70.